Samuel French Acting Edition

Six Rounds of Vengeance

by Qui Nguyen

SAMUELFRENCH.COM   SAMUELFRENCH.CO.UK

FOR PRODUCTION ENQUIRIES

UNITED STATES AND CANADA
Info@SamuelFrench.com
1-866-598-8449

UNITED KINGDOM AND EUROPE
Plays@SamuelFrench.co.uk
020-7255-4302

Each title is subject to availability from Samuel French, depending upon country of performance. Please be aware that *SIX ROUNDS OF VENGEANCE* may not be licensed by Samuel French in your territory. Professional and amateur producers should contact the nearest Samuel French office or licensing partner to verify availability.

MUSIC USE NOTE

Licensees are solely responsible for obtaining formal written permission from copyright owners to use copyrighted music in the performance of this play and are strongly cautioned to do so. If no such permission is obtained by the licensee, then the licensee must use only original music that the licensee owns and controls. Licensees are solely responsible and liable for all music clearances and shall indemnify the copyright owners of the play(s) and their licensing agent, Samuel French, against any costs, expenses, losses and liabilities arising from the use of music by licensees. Please contact the appropriate music licensing authority in your territory for the rights to any incidental music.

IMPORTANT BILLING AND CREDIT REQUIREMENTS

If you have obtained performance rights to this title, please refer to your licensing agreement for important billing and credit requirements.

SIX ROUNDS OF VENGEANCE received its world premiere Off Off Broadway by Vampire Cowboys at the New Ohio Theatre in New York City on April 24, 2015, under producer Abby Marcus; with scenic and lighting design by Nick Francone, sound design by Shane Rettig, costume design by Kristina Makowski, puppet design by David Valentine, multimedia design by Matthew Tennie, fight direction by Qui Nguyen, and stage management by Jeanne Travis. The director was Robert Ross Parker. The cast was as follows:

MALCOLM. . . . . .Sheldon Best

JESS . . . . .Jamie Dunn

DINGO/BIRDMAN/NATHANIEL/DON DIEGO. . . . . .Jon Hoche

LUCKY. . . . . .Tom Myers

DRUNK GIRL/OWL/GABBY. . . . . Nicky Schmidlein

CHARACTERS

JESS:	Badass cowgirl, seeking revenge for her fallen sister
LUCKY:	Jess' strongman sidekick who has an evil secret
MALCOLM:	English cowboy seeking revenge for his fallen lover
GABBY:	Jess' sweet sister turned bloodthirsty killer
OWL:	A corrupt French lawman, one of The Devils
DINGO:	A corrupt lawman, one of The Devils
DRUNK GIRL:	Dingo's drunk girlfriend
NATHANIEL:	Malcolm's ex-lover turned insane henchman
DON DIEGO:	A famous Spanish swordman who trains Jess
BIRDMAN:	A client of Owl's

Recommended Multi-Cast Breakdown for 2f/3m

1. **JESS**

2. **LUCKY**

3. **GABBY, OWL, DRUNK GIRL**

4. **MALCOLM**

5. **DINGO, NATHANIEL, DON DIEGO, BIRDMAN**

SETTING

A Post-Apocalyptic Las Vegas renamed "Lost Vegas."

PROLOGUE

(In the dark…)

JESS. *(Calling out.)* CHRISTIAN TOLSON, I'M CALLING YOU OUT!

> *(Lights up on badass cowgirl* **JESS**.*)*
>
> *(***DINGO*** stumbles in with a* **DRUNK GIRL** *on his arm.)*

DINGO. What do you want?

JESS. You Christian Tolson AKA Dingo the Butcher?

DINGO. What if I am?

> *(***JESS*** opens up her duster to show she's brandishing Japanese steel.)*

JESS. If you are, then we got business needs handling.

DRUNK GIRL. Girl, are you crazy? Do you not know who he is?

He's one of The Devils.

You ain't got a chance against no –

> *(***JESS*** backhands the* **DRUNK GIRL***. She screams and cries and dramatically runs away.)*

JESS. One year ago, your posse kidnapped and killed a girl named Gabby December.

DINGO. I don't recall killing no Gabby December. But then again, we bury bodies all the goddamn time. Sorry if I don't keep up on all their names.

JESS. Wrong answer.

> *(***JESS*** pulls out her blade.)*
>
> *(***DINGO*** pulls out a weapon of his own.)*

DINGO. Alright, cowgirl. You want to party? Then let's party.

> *(Suddenly **DINGO** attacks!)*
>
> *(Swords clash, a back and forth battle, but in the end – **JESS** stabs **DINGO** in the torso.)*
>
> *(He falls to his knees.)*

Little girl, you have no idea what kinda hell you just unleashed. When the rest of The Devils hear about this, we're gonna come kill your ass.

> *(**JESS** pulls out a gun and points it at his skull.)*

JESS. That's what I'm counting on.

> *(Blam!)*
>
> *(**JESS** suddenly breaks from her badass persona.)*

Oh my god oh my god oh my god, that worked!

> *(**JESS**, realizing, she's acting super "girly," shakes it off and reverts back to being…)*

I mean…of course that worked.

That's one.

Three to go.

> *(Projection: Six Rounds of Vengeance.)*

One

(Projection: Chapter one: In the beginning...)

(Spotlight on JESS.*)*

JESS. *(Addressing the audience.)* Howdy, I'm badass Jess December and welcome to my tale of death, destruction, and bloodshed. Welcome to my badass story of badass revenge. This is gonna be badass.

> *(*JESS*'s right hand man and BFF,* LUCKY, *enters. Though he's a large cowboy, he has a softness to his eyes. He also gives off a nervous energy, much akin to a scared bunny. A very big scared bunny.)*

LUCKY. Jess! Jess!

JESS. What is it, Luck?

LUCKY. Pissed off cowboy coming our way! He's walking fast and walking determined.

JESS. That was quick.

> *(*JESS *hands* LUCKY *the sword she got from* DINGO.*)*

Get into character!

> *(*JESS *and* LUCKY *try several different "badass poses" together, finally landing on something sufficiently "badass" on their third attempt.)*
>
> *(We now see the approaching cowboy. He walks slow, steady, and determined. We don't see his eyes, but we can tell by the way he walks he's not a man to be messed with.)*
>
> *(He enters.)*

MALCOLM. Oi. You two! I heard what you did to Dingo the Butcher.

JESS. *(Speaking like a badass cowboy.)* Was that us? Did we do that?

LUCKY. I don't like Dingos.

MALCOLM. I need words with you.

JESS. Is that right?

MALCOLM. You two just signed your own death certificates —

> (**LUCKY** *grabs a drink and tosses it at* **MALCOLM**.)
>
> (**MALCOLM** *dodges, but not before* **LUCKY** *attacks him.*)
>
> (*But before* **LUCKY** *can do any harm,* **MALCOLM** *already has his blade pointed at* **LUCKY***'s chest.*)

MALCOLM Alright, jolly green, calm down. I'm not here to fight you.

LUCKY. Got a funny way of showing it.

MALCOLM. What I was trying to say before you so rudely attacked me was — you two just signed your own death certificates IF you don't get some help on your side. I'm that help.

LUCKY. And why should we trust you?

MALCOLM. Well, for one, if I wanted — you'd both be dead right now. And the fact that I ain't slicing and dicing your crazy redneck bums should be an indication that I'm not trying or motivated in killing either one of you.

JESS. What do you think, Luck?

LUCKY. I don't like him.

JESS. Yeah, but you don't like nobody.

LUCKY. It's safer that way.

MALCOLM. Shooting Dingo Tolson is a declaration of war against The Devils.

JESS. Yeah, we know that.

MALCOLM. And if you can't beat me, there's no way you got a chance against The Devils.

JESS. What makes you think you can beat us?

MALCOLM. Is it your blade against my neck?

JESS. You do know what they say about guns and knife fights, right?

> (**JESS** *reveals she had her six-shooter pointed at him the whole time.*)

Lucky for you, I only use this when I'm killing Devils. This is my Devil-killing gun – if you're a Devil, I'd kill you – thus the name: The Devil-killing gun.

MALCOLM. You two twits don't know shit, do you?

JESS. Why's he talking to me like I did something stupid?

LUCKY. Why are you talking to her like she's stupid?

MALCOLM. Devils don't die by bullets. Only thing stands a chance against them is steel. Guns don't do diddly.

JESS. How do you know so much about them?

MALCOLM. Cause I used to be one of them. (Don't shoot me!)

LUCKY. Who are you?

MALCOLM. The name's Price. Malcolm Price. And if you want a chance at surviving this night, you now listen to me.

> (Cut to…)

> (During the follow monologue, we see the story of "The Devils" unfold on the back wall as either an elaborate shadow-play or animated sequence showing the silhouettes of cowboys [The Devils] and vampires [The Long Tooth Gang] do battle.)

JESS. (Addressing the audience.) Right. You may need some backstory. Years ago, as the world went to shit after the great big war, towns out west began closing their borders.

The Long Tooth Gang, a psychotic crew of evildoers were wreaking senseless violence all over the former US of A and everyone – and I mean everyone – was scared their town would be next. Five years ago, that fear became a reality here in Lost Vegas. People began disappearing, bloodstained streets became a common sight, and soon it would be that anyone caught outside after nightfall had guaranteed themselves a death sentence. That is until four masked lawmen rose up among our people and went to war against The Long

Tooths. And in one blood-soaked evening, The Devils took back our town.

> *(In the shadow-play, we see The Devils slay all the Long Tooth Gang.)*

But that was five years ago...

Now those same Devils who we once called our protectors are now our captors...

> *(Projection: One Year Earlier...)*

> *(Lights come up revealing a pretty little lass named* **GABBY**.*)*

> *(She's waiting nervously outside with a satchel and flashlight.)*

> *(A younger* **LUCKY** *sneaks on stage.)*

LUCKY. Psst.

GABBY. Where's Jess?

LUCKY. She ain't coming.

GABBY. What do you mean she ain't coming? What did you say to her?

LUCKY. I didn't say nuthin'.

GABBY. You didn't tell her we were going?

LUCKY. No.

GABBY. I ain't going anywhere without her.

LUCKY. Good, then don't. This is crazy. You know the rules. We're not supposed to be out at night. And we're definitely not supposed to leave the town walls.

GABBY. Jason, we're gonna be fine.

LUCKY. But The Devils –

GABBY. The Devils are all but a figment of our imaginations these days.

LUCKY. They ain't figments. They're still out there. I know it.

GABBY. Bullshit.

LUCKY. What about Dingo and Owl?

GABBY. Dingo's a town drunk and Owl's crazy. There ain't no proof they're really who they say they are.

LUCKY. But the stories –

GABBY. I'm telling you The Devils took off a long time ago. There ain't no one out there guarding our borders. For all we know, they've rode off, saved Los Angeles, and are now enjoying umbrella drinks on some beach.

LUCKY. I love you, Gabby December, but you're wrong. I was outside the night The Devils saved our town. The same night you and your sister found me and took me in. I seen firsthand what they did. They're protecting us. And as long as we follow their laws, they'll keep doing that.

GABBY. I know you saw them all those years back, but that don't mean they're still here.

LUCKY. Okay, fine, suppose you're right and they have left, do we also count on hoping that The Long Tooth Gang have also disappeared?

GABBY. That gang only attacks big cities. We just don't go to no big cities.

LUCKY. Then where?

GABBY. The woods, the mountains, the ocean. There's a lot of world out there where we can start over in.

LUCKY. I can't, Gabby.

GABBY. And I can't stay here any longer. We're wasting away here. I made up my mind – I'd rather die out there fighting toward becoming "a something" than spend another day longer just sitting here safely withering away as "a nothing."

LUCKY. Let's just wait 'til we can talk to Jess about it together, alright? Please. For me.

GABBY. I knew you were gonna do this.

LUCKY. You knew I was gonna do what?

GABBY. Jason –

>   (GABBY *walks up and gives* LUCKY *a soft, but very meaningful kiss.*)

Take care of Jess, okay? She's the one you're really in love with anyhow.

LUCKY. What?

(GABBY knees LUCKY in the balls.)

GABBY. Bye, baby.

(GABBY hightails it.)

(LUCKY pulls himself up off the ground.)

LUCKY. No! Gabby! Stop!

(LUCKY runs off after her.)

(Cut to…)

(Movement Sequence: We see GABBY running away through the night. We see her make distance between herself and LUCKY. She passes the "city wall" and into the cold desert…where it's dark… unusually dark…and she's all alone.)

(GABBY takes a moment and she closes her eyes, taking in a deep breath and enjoying the fact that she's finally free.)

(Until she hears something scurrying past her in the dark.)

(She shines a flashlight over in that direction, but there's nothing.)

GABBY. Hello? Jason, is that you?

(More scurrying.)

(She flings her flashlight over, but nothing.)

Jay?

(She slowly pans her flashlight and it quickly passes a masked devil [NATHANIEL].)

NATHANIEL. Naughty naughty.

GABBY. Oh God!

(She tries to run away, but NATHANIEL leaps on her, knocking her flashlight out.)

No, no, no! Please.

(GABBY lets out a loud scream as she's pulled into the darkness.)

JESS. The next morning, I found Lucky – bloodstained and beaten. The Devils had taken my sister and left him barely alive to remind us all what happens when you break the laws.

Laws we once believed protected us. Laws that in truth were only there to imprison us.

But that's why I'm here today.

To free us all.

> *(Cut to...)*

MALCOLM. I can't believe you called out Dingo like you did.

JESS. Killed Dingo.

MALCOLM. You know how long I been tracking him? He was supposed to lead me back to their leader, but now...damn, man!

JESS. Well, now, their leader is gonna come to us. You're welcome.

MALCOLM. Genius, their leader isn't going to come just because you pissed off one of his boys.

JESS. I didn't piss off one of his boys. I killed one of his boys.

MALCOLM. That bloke ain't dead.

JESS. The big ol' hole in his head would suggest otherwise.

MALCOLM. You're naive at best, an idiot otherwise. You don't know anything about anything.

JESS. You know what I don't know? What I don't know is why, since you admitted that you used to be one of them, I shouldn't just put a bullet into your pretty little face right now.

> (**JESS** *pulls out her pistol and points it at* **MALCOLM**.)

MALCOLM. Well, for one, you're gonna need me if you want a chance against the rest of them.

Two, I wasn't with The Devils when your sister died.

And three –

(**MALCOLM** *slyly strips her of her gun and points it back at her.*)

I don't know how you can use your gun when I have it.

JESS. Man!

MALCOLM. Baby, you might think you fly, but you ain't superfly.

JESS. Gimme that back.

Please.

Pretty please?

With sugar on top?

(**MALCOLM** *hands her back her piece.*)

What's your beef with The Devils anyhow? Are you just mad that they fired you?

MALCOLM. My beef is the same as yours. They took someone I loved. So I'm here to pay them back in pain. Girl, listen, you can either fight me or you can save that fight for the blokes who really deserve some killing. You struck one of their own today, that means they're gonna be coming to you hard and fast when that sun goes down. You and I got a common enemy. Let us work together. Otherwise, we're all gonna die.

(**JESS** *suddenly grabs* **MALCOLM** *and starts kissing him.*)

(*He pushes her away.*)

What are you doing?

JESS. What am I doing? You kissed me.

MALCOLM. No, I didn't. You grabbed my head.

JESS. After you leaned in.

MALCOLM. I was yelling at you.

JESS. Maybe with your mouth, but your eyes were saying something different.

MALCOLM. Oh yeah, what do you think they were saying?

(**JESS** *gets in his face.*)

JESS. Clearly something naughty.

In French.

Thus why I kissed you that way.

MALCOLM. Is that what you think?

LUCKY. *(Offstage.)* Hey!

> (**LUCKY** *enters with weapons as* **JESS** *and* **MALCOLM** *immediately separate.*)

Hey?

Um…

I cleaned all the burrs off your blade, Jess.

JESS. Thanks, Luck.

> (**LUCKY** *looks at both of them who can't seem to make eye contact with him.*)

LUCKY. So. Okay. What's the plan?

MALCOLM. Well, you shot Dingo, the weakest of the four.

LUCKY. You mean five.

MALCOLM. Well, not counting my retired ass, there's four. Two who patrol the streets, two who patrol the borders. Dingo and Owl hang here in town, so I suggest we take out Owl now while we still have the element of surprise on our side. The other two will come running once they don't get their check-ins from their counterparts here inside the wall.

JESS. There's a thing happening at the old burnt up Bellagio right now. If Owl's gonna be anywhere, it's gonna be there.

LUCKY. Um, are you sure about this, Jess? Shooting Dingo is one thing, going after Owl with whoever this guy is – no offense – paints a different kind of target on our backs.

JESS. Yes, I'm sure. My sister deserves justice.

LUCKY. But –

JESS. No. We're doing this.

LUCKY. Alright.

MALCOLM. Let's go make some evil.

(**MALCOLM** *goes to give a fist bump as* **JESS** *slaps it.*)

JESS. Sorry.

(*Cut to…*)

(**OWL**, *a sexy, masked singer, is dancing and singing for a seated cowboy who's dressed overly "badass" in all sorts of feathery attire. She speaks with a French accent.*)

OWL. You must be one dangerous cowboy, no?

BIRDMAN. Let's just say, no one pisses off the birdman without getting pissed on.

OWL. That's…ew.

BIRDMAN. Um. Maybe I should use a better catch phrase… Um, no one poops on the birdman without getting pooped on.

OWL. Perhaps you should stick to being the strong, silent type, yes?

BIRDMAN. That's right. That's me. Strong and silent.

(**OWL** *continues flirting with* **BIRDMAN** *as we see on a "split screen" the arriving* **JESS**, **LUCKY**, *and* **MALCOLM** *on horseback.*)

JESS. Why are you scowling?

LUCKY. I'm not scowling. I'm looking intimidating.

JESS. That's supposed to be intimidating?

LUCKY. Do I not look intimidating?

JESS. For such a big guy, you do not project intimidating very well at all.

LUCKY. What do I project?

JESS. Cuddly?

LUCKY. Stop it, Jess.

JESS. So why are you trying to look intimidating?

LUCKY. You don't think it's funny that as soon as you whacked Dingo, Skinny John Shaft over there suddenly shows up and starts bossing us around?

JESS. I got my eye on him.

LUCKY. That's what I'm worried about. That ain't the kinda eye that's gonna keep us from getting stabbed in the back.

JESS. What's that supposed to mean?

LUCKY. I just don't trust him. I think he might be the real bad guy here.

MALCOLM. You two do know that I can hear every word you're saying.

LUCKY. What?

MALCOLM. If y'all are done talking shit behind my back, we're here.

> *(They all dismount their steeds.)*

(Calling out.) OWL THE HEARTLESS!

> *(On the other side of the stage,* **OWL** *stops dancing. Both her and* **BIRDMAN** *turn to the door.)*

We're calling you out.

Or we're coming in.

> *(In the bar…)*

BIRDMAN. Don't you move a sexy muscle, baby. I got this.

> *(**BIRDMAN** stands up, opens his coat, and reveals his impressive array of weapons.)*
>
> *(He pulls out a knife and a machete.)*

Let's see them stop –

> *(**JESS**, **MALCOLM**, and **LUCKY** enter and raise their weapons at* **BIRDMAN**.)*

Or on the other hand…

> *(**BIRDMAN** runs away!)*

OWL. Dammit. And I was going to eat him later.

MALCOLM. Lila Boudreau or should I say Owl the Heartless, we're here with the mind to make a mess.

OWL. Officer Price. It's been a long time. We all assumed you had died. Fortunately for our beloved Nathaniel, you are still with us. He'll be so happy.

JESS. Wait, she's Owl? Not the dude with all the feathers? Well, that's confusing.

OWL. And who are your friends?

JESS. I'm Jess December, bitch. You Devils killed my sister!

> (JESS *pulls out her gun –.*)

MALCOLM. Don't!

> (*– And shoots* OWL.)

> (OWL, *however, catches the bullet. And drops it at their feet.*)

I told you that wouldn't work.

JESS. Okay then. Violence it is.

> (JESS *leaps passed* MALCOLM *and attacks* OWL.)

MALCOLM. Stop!

> (*An elaborate fight ensues beginning with* OWL *versus* JESS, *which then escalates into a brawl between* OWL, JESS, *and* MALCOLM.)

> (LUCKY *is taken out early in the fight when he charges, trips, and runs his head into a wall.*)

> (When JESS *and* MALCOLM *get* OWL *cornered, her eyes suddenly turn red.*)

OWL. Okay, you two, I did not want to mess up my nice clothes like this, but you've given me no choice.

MALCOLM. Get back.

> (*With the help of lights and sound,* OWL *begins transforming into a werewolf.*)

JESS. What in the hell?

> (JESS *pulls out her pistol and points it.*)

MALCOLM. Put that gun down. It won't do anything. You have to cut her throat!

(They attack. The souped-up **OWL** *begins beating the snot out of* **MALCOLM** *and* **JESS**.*)*

(They don't stand a chance.)

(She gets **JESS** *cornered.)*

(Seeing his friend in danger, **LUCKY** *leaps to his feet and charges* **OWL**.*)*

LUCKY. No, stay away from her.

OWL. You're pretty. Just like your sister. Let me show you what we did to her.

*(***OWL** *goes to bite* **JESS** *in the face until* **LUCKY** *grabs her. He suddenly turns very serious.)*

LUCKY. No! I told you to stay away!

*(***LUCKY** *lifts* **OWL** *into the air by the throat.)*

OWL. You! Would you really trade me in for her? HER?!

LUCKY. Yes.

(He breaks her neck.)

*(***OWL***'s body goes limp and falls to the ground.)*

(Her body thudding the ground freaks out **LUCKY**, *who immediately backs off and cowers from what he just did.)*

JESS. Okay. What in the HELL did she just turn into?

MALCOLM. Goddamn, you're even stronger than you look. Looks like we got ourselves a secret weapon.

JESS. Lucky, you okay?

LUCKY. I've never done something like that before.

JESS. It's okay, hon. It's okay. You saved me.

*(***JESS** *hugs* **LUCKY** *as* **MALCOLM** *goes to slice* **OWL***'s throat.)*

MALCOLM. Goodbye, Lila.

(As he runs his blade across her neck, lights, sounds, and projections explode into a fury as the soul of a demon is released from **OWL***'s body.*

*Her body stiffens and arches as the demon is
vanquished and she suddenly falls limp.)*

JESS. Okay, what was that? How the hell was she able to do
that?

*(A worn-out **MALCOLM** reaches into his coat and
pulls out a flask. He takes a swig.)*

MALCOLM. Can't you two prats do math?

How do you think The Devils were able to push out the
Long Tooth Gang so easily? This is how. They turned
themselves into something just as bloodthirsty as their
enemies.

JESS. They turned themselves into Long Tooths?

MALCOLM. No. Worse. Much much worse.

(He takes another swig.)

*(A spotlight falls onto **MALCOLM**.)*

(Projection: Five Years Ago...)

*(During the following monologue, we see
MALCOLM's story re-enacted in the background by
the cast. All the actors wear bandanas across their
faces to turn themselves neutral.)*

It had been weeks since the Long Tooths had broken
through our walls. We had tried our best to fight them
off, but we quickly discovered that the Long Tooths
were more than just outlaws, they were something else
– something we had never seen before. They drank
blood, they could rip you apart with their bare hands,
and they didn't die when you shot them. We had no
chance, that is until a mysterious masked stranger
walked into our precinct and claimed he had a secret
to making us stronger, faster, and better than the beasts
we were fighting. However, it would demand from us a
small sacrifice.

*(In a very ceremonial way, a masked Walker
[**LUCKY**] brings in a gagged girl [actress playing
JESS] and tosses her center stage.)*

"Eat of this flesh," he told us. "Eat of it and you will be bestowed the power of the Skin Walker. We will be able to transform into any beast we can imagine to conquer any foe that comes before us. EAT!"

VICTIM. No no no –

(Walker and his Devils bite into her!)

Aaaaaah!

*(Blackout on the background players. Now only a spotlight on **MALCOLM** alone onstage.)*

MALCOLM. You have to understand that we were rapidly losing ground, we were desperate. So many of us had lost so many of our loved ones already.

My fellow officers Christian and Lila ate of it and transformed themselves into beasts. I did not. I was too scared. But Walker was right, they indeed became stronger, faster, and incredibly powerful – but what Walker didn't warn was now they had also grown crueler, heartless, and suddenly unwavering in their obedience to their new masked leader. And when I refused to join them, they killed my lover. This is what we're up against.

*(**MALCOLM** takes another swig.)*

And to be honest with you, though we may stand a chance against Dingo and Owl, when Walker comes to town, we're all gonna die.

Two

(Projection: Chapter Two: Personal attacks.)

(Projection: Five Years Earlier...)

(JESS *sits on their porch, standing guard with a gun by her side.)*

(GABBY *enters.)*

JESS. What are you still doing up?

GABBY. Couldn't sleep.

JESS. You should try.

GABBY. But I can't –

JESS. Whatever. Do what you want. But it's still your shift in three hours.

GABBY. Okay.

JESS. Okay.

GABBY. It's quiet out.

JESS. It is.

GABBY. Do you really think the Long Tooth Gang is gone?

JESS. That's what our new friend just told us. Hard to believe it though.

GABBY. He's still pretty banged up.

JESS. He'll get better. It'll be good to have another set of hands around.

GABBY. He's cute.

JESS. Stop.

GABBY. He is.

JESS. How do you do that?

GABBY. Do what?

JESS. Think about unimportant stuff like that when the world is literally falling apart around us?

GABBY. I don't know. It's better than just sitting around thinking about dying all the time, right?

JESS. Right.

GABBY. ...

JESS. …

GABBY. Hey. What do you want to be when you grow up?

JESS. What?

GABBY. What do you wanna be when you grow up?

JESS. You're kidding me with that question, right?

GABBY. It's just a question.

JESS. It's a dumb question.

GABBY. You asked me how I can think about stuff other than the world falling apart around me, this is how. I pretend the world is still okay. So what do you want to be.

JESS. Really.

GABBY. It's just a hypothetical.

JESS. Well, if I could make a time machine that could travel us back to a time when the world still had things like electricity and motorized vehicles and regular people didn't have to worry on the daily about being murdered by morning… I guess I'd want to be an accountant.

GABBY. An accountant?

JESS. Yeah. Something boring. But safe. That's what I'd want to be.

GABBY. Safe sounds good.

> *(Suddenly, there's a faint scream far away from them.)*
>
> *(It chills the air as both the girls become immediately very still and very quiet.)*
>
> *(They wait for a time.)*
>
> *(They don't move or breathe until they know for a fact that whatever it was that caused that scream is long gone.)*
>
> *(And then they wait just a bit more.)*
>
> *(And then they breathe and are back into their normal trivial conversation.)*

GABBY Do you ever think of Mom or Dad?

JESS. Everyday. All the time.

GABBY. Me too.

I wish they were here.

JESS. Me too.

GABBY. We're going to be alright, right?

JESS. I don't know, Gabs. I honestly don't know. But as long as I'm alive, I promise I'm gonna do whatever I can to take care of you.

> (**GABBY** *puts her head on her sister's shoulder and closes her eyes.*)

Go to sleep, hon. I got this. No bad guys are gonna get you tonight. I promise.

> (**JESS** *strokes her sister's hair as she falls asleep.*)
>
> (*Projection: Present.*)
>
> (*Lights up on* **MALCOLM** *and* **LUCKY** *as they both individually patch up wounds from their fight with* **OWL**.)
>
> (**LUCKY** *drinks a beer as he watches* **MALCOLM** *dress a cut.*)

LUCKY. Stay away from her.

MALCOLM. What?

LUCKY. Stay away from Jess. I see the way you've been looking at her and I don't like it.

MALCOLM. And how have I been looking at her?

LUCKY. You know how you've been looking at her.

MALCOLM. No, describe it. I ain't quite sure.

LUCKY. You know. Lustfully.

MALCOLM. Lustfully?

LUCKY. Yeah.

MALCOLM. I'm not quite picturing it. How does lustfully look?

LUCKY. You know how lustfully looks.

MALCOLM. Son, it's not like I walk around with a mirror when I make faces. I don't know what kinda faces I make, so I'm not sure which of those faces are the ones that seem to be offending you, partner.

LUCKY. The lustful one.

MALCOLM. Yeah, I don't know what you're talking about. Guess you're gonna have to deal with it because I must got "Resting Lustful Face."

LUCKY. Shut up, it looks like this.

> (**LUCKY** *tries to give a "lustful look."*)

MALCOLM. That's lustful?

LUCKY. Yeah.

MALCOLM. Let me see that again.

> (**LUCKY** *makes the impression again.*)

That looks more like constipation to me. Yes, I will try to stop looking constipated at Jess.

LUCKY. Just stay away from her!

MALCOLM. Besides being a master impersonator, you're also quite the detective.

LUCKY. What's that supposed to mean?

MALCOLM. I'm not interested in your friend. Not in that way. Now now. Not ever.

Because, see, there's one particular ingredient here in this jealousy stew that you're brewing that doesn't quite add up.

LUCKY. What's that?

MALCOLM. I'm gay.

LUCKY. You're what?

MALCOLM. And not as in "happy" either. I mean gay as in homosexual as in queer as in one beautiful badass unicorn bursting with rainbow fruit flavors...that loves doing dudes.

LUCKY. So you're a gay black English samurai cowboy?

MALCOLM. Yeah.

LUCKY. That's a lot of labels to wear.

MALCOLM. It is.

So?

LUCKY. So what?

MALCOLM. So don't you think you should be doing some apologizing?

LUCKY. I'm sorry you're gay?

MALCOLM. No!

LUCKY. English?

MALCOLM. For suggesting that my motivations in this endeavor has been anything less than noble.

LUCKY. Oh. Okay.

MALCOLM. Also for suggesting that I'm the bad guy.

LUCKY. Heh.

MALCOLM. What's "heh" supposed to mean?

LUCKY. "Heh" 'cause I still ain't so sure you ain't gonna wanna kill us at the end of the day. "Heh" cause I don't trust anyone who "used to be" a Devil. And "Heh" cause, frankly, I still don't like you.

> (**MALCOLM** and **LUCKY** are in a stare down.)
>
> (**JESS** enters.)

JESS. Is that testosterone I smell?

Okay, boys, which one's bigger?

No, go ahead. Whip them out, which one's bigger?

> (**MALCOLM** and **LUCKY** disengage from the other.)

Okay. We still have thirty minutes left till sundown. You sure they're gonna be coming for us this quickly?

MALCOLM. I have no doubt.

JESS. So what can you tell us about the last two Devils?

MALCOLM. Don't worry about Nathaniel. I got him.

The real threat is Chief Walker. Not only can he transform into animals, he can also transform into monsters. Monsters like the Wendigo.

JESS. What the hell is a Wendigo?

MALCOLM. Trust me, you don't wanna see.

LUCKY. Jess, this guy sounds dangerous.

MALCOLM. He is.

LUCKY. Are you sure you're ready for this?

JESS. Absolutely. I've spent the last year preparing for this fight. I'm ready.

> *(Spotlight on JESS.)*
>
> *(Projection: One Year Earlier...)*
>
> *(She pulls out her blade and starts practicing. She's awful at it.)*
>
> *(As JESS works on her swordwork, DON DIEGO, an older Spanish man, enters and watches her. He uses a cane and wears an eyepatch.)*

DON DIEGO. *Señorita,* may I offer you some light advice on your swordplay?

JESS. No thank you.

DON DIEGO. As a clearly very accomplished swordsman myself, observing your form, technique, and...body, I can assure you that my advice will greatly help you. They call me the fastest hands in the West.

JESS. You?

DON DIEGO. May I demonstrate?

> *(DON DIEGO raises his cane like a sword.)*

It is an honor to have this dance.

> *(JESS rolls her eyes and falls into an en garde.)*
>
> *(She steps forward and he immediately knocks her blade out of her hand.)*

JESS. What the hell?

DON DIEGO. As you can see, *señorita,* I am as swift as I am handsome.

> *(JESS picks up her sword.)*

JESS. Again –

> *(DON DIEGO again knocks the blade out of her hand before she can even truly engage.)*

Dammit! Fine, okay, I get that you're –

> *(In the middle of her sentence, JESS suddenly attacks without warning. This time, she is able to take a handful of attacks at the old Spanish swordsman who easily dodges her cuts and whips her on the butt with his cane. He shoots her a smile.)*

> *(This pisses off JESS and she take an angry attack at DON DIEGO; he, however, binds her blade into a corps-a-corps and steals a kiss from JESS as well as her blade.)*

DON DIEGO. It looks like you lose.

JESS. Give me back my blade.

DON DIEGO. But of course.

> *(He whips the sword to her and she catches it with a flourish.)*

JESS. Who are you?

DON DIEGO. My name's Don Diego de la Vega. I am a great swordsman…who happens to no longer have a sword.

JESS. What happened to it?

DON DIEGO. I lost it in a fight against one of *Los Diablos* of this town.

JESS. Is that how you lost that eye?

DON DIEGO. It is.

JESS. Do you teach?

DON DIEGO. Oh no. Not anymore. Not ever. Not since… Catherine.

JESS. I'll get your sword back if you do.

DON DIEGO. Against *Los Diablos*?

JESS. Yes.

> *(**DON DIEGO** laughs at the idea.)*

DON DIEGO. You would die.

JESS. Maybe I will. Maybe I won't. But this fight *will* happen.

(JESS starts practicing her swordplay again. It is still awful. She even drops it.)

DON DIEGO. Wait!

What kind of gentleman would I be to say no to such a pretty *señorita?* Meet me here in the morning and we will begin your training. Wear something…tight.

(Cut to…)

*(Music like the Jackson 5's **"DANCING MACHINE"** begins playing.)*

(Montage sequence: **DON DIEGO** *trains* **JESS** *in the art of combat.)*

(Two actors with muletas [bullfighter flags] stand adjacent and sweep the action to create cinematic "cuts" as the montage progresses. We see the evolution of the training montage. As the training begin, **JESS** *is terrible.* **DON DIEGO** *easily beats her attacks and ends each sequence with another whip to the butt with his cane.)*

(As it continues though, she gets better, finally using one of **DON DIEGO***'s own techniques against him to steal his cane from him.)*

(In the last sequence, he smiles in approval as she gives him back his cane. However as she does, he tricks her and whips her sword out of her hand like he did when they met, however this time she falls into a surprising capoeira defense that dodges all his attacks. In the end, she's able to steal his cane from him once again, and this time she ends the sequence by whipping him in the butt with it.)

(He nods in approval.)

(Cut to…)

DON DIEGO Not bad. Not bad at all.

There is nothing left for me to teach you now. If you wish to get better at the blade, you must now test your skills against a real opponent.

JESS. So I'm ready?

DON DIEGO. No one is ever truly ready to face *Los Diablos*. But you are better than you were. That will have to do.

JESS. Thank you, Diego.

DON DIEGO. I have one last thing for you

JESS. What's that?

> (**DON DIEGO** *removes a necklace he is wearing and gives it to* **JESS**.)

DON DIEGO. It's a necklace.

JESS. It's a...tooth necklace.

DON DIEGO. I did not say it was a nice necklace.

JESS. You know I'm vegan, right? I think wearing the teeth of something dead is equally as gross as eating something dead.

DON DIEGO. Don't be so negative.

JESS. So is it magical or something?

DON DIEGO. Why? Just because I'm a handsome old Spanish swordmaster with a sexy accent, everything I give you has to be magical? That's a bit culturally insensitive, don't you think?

JESS. I'm so sorry, I didn't mean –

DON DIEGO. I was joking. Of course it is magical.

JESS. Really? It is?!

DON DIEGO. I was kidding.

JESS. So it's not magical?

DON DIEGO. Why would I give you something not magical?

JESS. What?

DON DIEGO. It's magical.

JESS. It is?

DON DIEGO. No.

JESS. No?

DON DIEGO. Sí.

JESS. Is it or is it not?

DON DIEGO. I'm not sure.

JESS. You know what? It's nice. Thank you. I really appreciate having something's teeth around my neck.

DON DIEGO. See. I knew you would love it.

> (**JESS** *notices a gun on* **DON DIEGO** *and points to it.*)

JESS. Hey. What's this?

DON DIEGO. Oh, it's nothing of any importance.

JESS. Does it still work?

DON DIEGO. It does. But it only has six bullets left in it.

JESS. Can I have it?

DON DIEGO. It is a relic of a time long passed.

JESS. Can I have it?

DON DIEGO. Of course.

It has been an honor teaching you, *Señorita*. You've made these last few months some of the best in my life.

JESS. Why are you making this sound so final?

DON DIEGO. You are about to start a war against *Los Diablos*. Don Diego De La Vega did not live this long by putting himself in the middle of such duels.

JESS. But there's no way out of Lost Vegas.

DON DIEGO. *Señorita*, there's always a way out.

> (**JESS** *and* **DON DIEGO** *hug.*)

If I may give you one last piece of advice before you head into this fight, leave no regrets behind.

> (**DON DIEGO** *stares at* **JESS**…*and then begins to lean.*)

JESS. Whoa.

DON DIEGO. What? You didn't think… I wasn't trying to – you mean…hey, look at that.

> (**DON DIEGO** *points to something behind* **JESS**.)

JESS. What?

> (*As she looks, he runs away.*)

(When she turns back and can't find him, she concludes –.)

Magic.

(Cut to…)

(Projection: Present.)

(**LUCKY** *is outside, keeping watch, hiding behind some sort of makeshift barricade.*)

(**JESS** *enters.*)

Hey.

LUCKY. Hey.

JESS. See anything yet?

LUCKY. Nope.

JESS. *(Calling out.)* Malcolm, do you see anything?

MALCOLM. *(Offstage.)* Shut! Up!

JESS. Sorry!

MALCOLM. *(Offstage.)* I said shut up! (Fuckin' white people.)

LUCKY. I don't want to do this, Jess.

JESS. You're just scared is all.

LUCKY. I don't wanna see you get hurt. You've been everything to me for so long.

JESS. Jason –

LUCKY. I need to tell you something.

JESS. What?

LUCKY. It's… I feel awful.

JESS. What is it?

LUCKY. Do you think…maybe…what you want to do here is maybe a bit…well, selfish?

JESS. What?

LUCKY. If we kill The Devils, who's to protect everyone from The Long Tooth Gang.

JESS. There's no more Long Tooth Gang.

LUCKY. Or maybe we've been so safe inside these walls that we've taken for granted what The Devils have actually done for us. Listen, Jess, this isn't just about you and

Gabby. It's about everyone here in Vegas. Maybe we still need their protection.

JESS. Where is this coming from?

LUCKY. I just… I care about you. I just don't want to see you hurt.

JESS. I care about you too, Luck.

LUCKY. No. I mean… I care about you.

JESS. Oh.

LUCKY. I'm sorry. I just – I think what you're about to do is going to change everything and I don't know if I'm ready for that change.

JESS. Luck…

I care about you too.

LUCKY. …

JESS. Look at me. You and me. We have each other. That's all that's important. We'll be fine.

LUCKY. Sure.

JESS. Hey, we're going to be okay. I promise. Now hang tight. I'm going to go back to my post.

(JESS *leaves.*)

(JESS *returns.*)

Just one last thing –

(*She kisses* LUCKY. *He kisses her back. It's a very sweet moment.*)

Just in case.

LUCKY. Jess…

JESS. We'll talk more about this later.

(JESS *leaves.*)

LUCKY. That's what I'm worried about.

MALCOLM. Goddamn! Shut! Up!

Three

(Projection: Chapter Three: Not all dead things stay dead.)

(Projection: One year earlier…)

*(Lights come up on **NATHANIEL** dragging in a gagged, kicking and screaming girl [**GABBY**].)*

*(**NATHANIEL** speaks and sings with an English accent.)*

NATHANIEL.
HUSH LITTLE BABY DON'T SAY A WORD.
MAMA'S GONNA BUY YOU A MOCKINGBIRD.
AND IF THAT MOCKINGBIRD DON'T SCREAM.
MAMA'S GONNA RIP OFF BOTH ITS WINGS
AND IF THAT MOCKINGBIRD WON'T DIE
MAMA'S GONNA POKE OUT BOTH ITS EYES
AND IF THAT MOCKINGBIRD WON'T GO
WE'LL FRY IT UP AND EAT IT WHOLE…

Shhhh shhhh.

Quiet, love. There's nothing to be afraid of – well, actually that's a bit of a lie, now isn't it? There's quite a bit to be afraid of – but the situation being what it is, kicking and screaming like you are isn't going to do you much good either way.

I know, love, this is not how you were planning to have your final hours of life play out. But then again, maybe it is, maybe this is exactly how you wanted to close out the final chapter of your sad pathetic life. I mean, why else would you tempt fate like you did? Is one rule really that hard to follow? We gave you lot one simple rule to follow for your own protection, yet here we are. What was that rule, love?

GABBY. No one leaves town.

NATHANIEL. No one leaves town.

Yet where did I find you?

GABBY. Please. I didn't know –

NATHANIEL. I realize you thought we were make-believe. Some people just have to see the sausage being made no matter how bloody it may get.

> (GABBY *hits* NATHANIEL.)

> (NATHANIEL *enjoys it.*)

Mmm, yes. I like that.

GABBY. Stay away.

NATHANIEL. You look absolutely delicious. But unfortunately for me, Chief Walker has a different plan for you, love. So I'm not allowed to eat you whole. But that doesn't mean I can't have a small nibble. Come here.

GABBY. No!

> (GABBY *takes off running.*)

> (NATHANIEL *doesn't speed up his step, though. Instead, he begins skipping after her.*)

> (Movement Sequence: We see GABBY *running away from* NATHANIEL *through a dark forest.*)

> (She *leaps behind bushes, behind trees, dives into ditches, etc.*)

> (However *as hard as she runs, like a slasher movie monster,* NATHANIEL *[without running] is tight on her tail.*)

> (As NATHANIEL *nears,* GABBY *begins blindly sprinting through the woods until she slams face first into the torso of a very large man.*)

> (She *looks up and sees it's –.*)

GABBY. Jason!

LUCKY. Gabby. Are you alright?

GABBY. The Devils. They're real. You were right, you were so right.

LUCKY. It's okay, baby. It's okay. Just climb into my arms. I got you.

GABBY. Oh god, I so messed up. I just want to go home. I just want to go home.

LUCKY. Don't worry. I'll get you there.

> (**NATHANIEL** *enters.*)

GABBY. Oh God! Jason!

LUCKY. Don't worry. He won't hurt you.
Sit, doggy! Sit.

NATHANIEL. Are you serious with this doggy shite?

GABBY. What are you doing?

LUCKY. Sit!

> (*Like magic,* **NATHANIEL** *is "forced" to sit.*)

NATHANIEL. For fuck's sake.

> (**NATHANIEL** *sits.*)

GABBY. Why's he listening to you?

LUCKY. Now beg. BEG!

NATHANIEL. Oh please please, will you feed me?

LUCKY. Sorry, doggy. No kibble here.

> (**LUCKY**'s *eyes grow cold.*)

GABBY. Jason?

LUCKY. I'm sorry. This wouldn't have happened if I could've just kept you inside the wall.

GABBY. Lucky, what are you –

LUCKY. There's rules. If people found out that I let you break them, it'd be chaos.

GABBY. Let me?

LUCKY. I got no choice, baby. But at least this way, you're not going to die.

GABBY. What?

> (**LUCKY** *grabs* **GABBY** *by the face –.*)

Jason, let me go!

LUCKY. I'm going to make you strong.

> (*– And bites a chunk out of her cheek.*)

GABBY. Aaaaah!

> *(Blood sprays everywhere. He drops her as she writhes around in pain.)*

LUCKY. I'm sorry. That must hurt. But don't worry, you'll be better soon.

> *(A single spotlight falls on* **GABBY** *as she writhes in pain.* **LUCKY** *and* **NATHANIEL** *disappear in the darkness as* **GABBY** *continues to convulse in the spotlight.)*
>
> *(And then collapse.)*
>
> *(And then she is motionless.)*
>
> *(A beat begins. It's something slow and driving.)*
>
> *(As the beat continues,* **GABBY**'s *lifeless body begins to move again.)*
>
> *(She slowly pulls herself off the ground as the beat begins speeding up in tempo and volume.)*
>
> *(Finally, she's on her feet, but now her eyes have grown cold and an evil smirk emerges on her face.)*
>
> *(Blood drips from her lips.)*
>
> *(Projection: Present night…)*
>
> *(Suddenly the lights shift and this new rabid "evil"* **GABBY** *is standing in the middle of* **JESS**, **MALCOLM**, *and* **LUCKY**.)*

GABBY. Hey sissy.

> *(They immediately raise their weapons in surprise.)*

JESS. Oh God! Gabby?

GABBY. Did y'all make all this trouble just for me?

> *(***GABBY*** *pulls out two blades of her own.)*

Aw, you shouldn't have.

Come here and let me give you a big ol' kiss.

End of Act I

ACT II

Four

(Projection: Chapter Four: The enemy within.)

(Projection: Ten years earlier…)

(NATHANIEL is fumbling around, making his apartment perfectly romantic.)

MALCOLM. *(Offstage.)* Nathaniel, you in here?

(NATHANIEL quickly gets into a seductive position to greet his lover.)

NATHANIEL. Hey.

MALCOLM. Hey. What did you do to our living room? Did we lose power again?

NATHANIEL. Not unless the stereo suddenly started running on batteries.

*(NATHANIEL clicks the stereo on with a remote. A song like UB40's **"RED RED WINE"** begins playing.)*

MALCOLM. Oi, what's that? Are you trying to torture me?

NATHANIEL. Would you care for some wine, love?

MALCOLM. What?

NATHANIEL. Some red red wine, my love?

MALCOLM. Today our anniversary, is it?

NATHANIEL. No.

MALCOLM. Did you get a raise or something?

NATHANIEL. No.

MALCOLM. Then what is this all about?

NATHANIEL. I just thought something romantic would be nice.

MALCOLM. Awwww, babe. Not tonight. I'm just a bit knackered is all.

NATHANIEL. Oh.

MALCOLM. When I signed up for this job, I thought it'd be more adventurous.

NATHANIEL. Like chips?

MALCOLM. What?

NATHANIEL. Nevermind.

MALCOLM. But instead it's just walking around, handing out parking tickets all day.

NATHANIEL. Right.

MALCOLM. And the women here all think I'm a stripper just because of my accent – which I guess is a compliment – some old broad actually shoved a fiver down my pants today after I gave her directions. That was weird, but profitable.

NATHANIEL. You're not regretting that I brought you out here?

MALCOLM. No no no, Nathaniel. I love America. I do. I can't wait to get fat and start watching their version of football where no one actually uses their feet.

NATHANIEL. You don't have to work, you know. I make plenty.

MALCOLM. I told you when I met you, I make my own way.

NATHANIEL. I know, it's just –

MALCOLM. I'm good, love.

Which does not seem to be your state of being right now.

What's wrong?

NATHANIEL. It's nothing.

MALCOLM. It's not nothing. Are you upset that I'm not in the mood? We can still snog a bit if you want. I just have to crash soon is all.

NATHANIEL. It's fine.

MALCOLM. It's not fine. You're slumpy. The only time I see you this slumpy is when you're about to cry.

NATHANIEL. I don't cry.

MALCOLM. Not even at Morgan Freeman films?

Should we put *March of the Penguins* on to prove my point? Honestly, is today an anniversary on something I can't remember? Like the first time we did it?

NATHANIEL. Ha. Ha.

MALCOLM. You were so nervous. I honestly couldn't tell if that was due to you being slightly inexperienced or being slightly racist.

NATHANIEL. I'm not racist.

MALCOLM. "I've never been with a black bloke before. You're not going to hurt me, right? I'm so scared of your giant mandingo wang."

NATHANIEL. I never said that.

MALCOLM. You didn't need to, your eyes did.

NATHANIEL. Oh shut it!

MALCOLM. Scented candles? You can be such a poofta sometimes! Come here.

> (**MALCOLM** *give* **NATHANIEL** *a hug and notices a box in his pocket.*)

Now what's this?

NATHANIEL. OH GOD! Nothing!

MALCOLM. Well, obviously it's not nothing.

NATHANIEL. Give it here.

MALCOLM. No, what is it?

NATHANIEL. It's – well, me mum found my collector's edition Captain Justice Decoder ring and sent it to me.

MALCOLM. In a velvet box?

NATHANIEL. It's fake velvet.

MALCOLM. Hold on. This isn't –

NATHANIEL. No no no no NO!

MALCOLM. Get off me, you slag.

NATHANIEL. No!

> (**NATHANIEL** *grabs* **MALCOLM**. *They wrestle around a bit and* **NATHANIEL** *accidentally hurts* **MALCOLM**'s *wrist.*)

MALCOLM. Ow!

NATHANIEL. Oh God, I'm sorry!

> (**NATHANIEL** *lets him go. And* **MALCOLM** *smiles [He was faking being hurt].*)

MALCOLM. Really?

NATHANIEL. Look, it's just a toy. It's. Just. A. Toy.

> (**MALCOLM** *opens it.*)

MALCOLM. This is an engagement ring.

NATHANIEL. Would you believe Captain Justice is just a really fancy dresser?

MALCOLM. You were going to propose to me tonight.

NATHANIEL. Maybe.

MALCOLM. Oh.

NATHANIEL. Soooo…would it be safe now to ask you if you would –

MALCOLM. HAVE YOU LOST YOUR BLOODY MIND, MAN? WHAT WERE YOU THINKING?! You can't ask me to marry you! I can't marry you!

NATHANIEL. Fine. Okay. Just calm down.

MALCOLM. I had an awful day today. I was not prepared for this. And it's a Tuesday! Who in their right mind proposes on a Tuesday? It's the least romantic day of the week.

NATHANIEL. Malcolm, I'm sorry.

MALCOLM. You let me fuck up this day. This day, you let me fuck up. I will never ever forgive you!

NATHANIEL. Baby –

MALCOLM. Asshole!

> (**MALCOLM** *storms off.*)

NATHANIEL. Super.

> *(A moment passes.)*

> *(**MALCOLM** runs back in, grabs **NATHANIEL** and immediately kisses him.)*

What are you doing?

MALCOLM. Well, I thought it over. And since I decided I'm going to be spending the rest of my life with you, I thought a kiss would be in order.

NATHANIEL. So you're going to marry me?

MALCOLM. What makes you think I'd say no?

> *(**NATHANIEL** and **MALCOLM** kiss again.)*

May I have this first dance?

> *(The song from earlier comes back on as they dance. It's an earnest, soft, and romantic moment...)*

> *(Which slowly morphs back into the streets of Vegas as the rest of the actors enter the stage to help transform **MALCOLM** back into his fighting gear and the setting back into the violent streets of the west.)*

> *(Cut to...)*

GABBY. Aw, sissy, you shouldn't have.

Come here and let me give you a big ol' kiss.

> *(**GABBY** suddenly attacks. **JESS** is frozen, but **MALCOLM** leaps in the way to defend her.)*

> *(**MALCOLM** and **GABBY** fight. He knocks her down and puts her on point.)*

MALCOLM. Stay down. Do you hear me? STAY. DOWN!

GABBY. Aw, you're no fun.

> *(**NATHANIEL** enters.)*

NATHANIEL. I disagree.

MALCOLM. Nathaniel?

NATHANIEL. Hello there, love. I thought you weren't into the ladies. I guess we've all changed a bit since we last saw one another.

>   (GABBY *suddenly strikes the distracted* MALCOLM.)

>   (*Eventually,* MALCOLM *and* JESS *are able to fight the monsters back.*)

JESS. Gabby, please stop.

MALCOLM. They're not who they were. That's not your sister. He's not my Nathaniel.

GABBY. Would you really hurt me, sissy?

JESS. I… I can't do this. I can't…

>   (LUCKY *approaches.*)

LUCKY. Luckily, I can.

>   (LUCKY *pulls out his sword and in one large swoop, slices both…* JESS *and* MALCOLM.)

MALCOLM AND JESS. Agh!

>   (NATHANIEL *and* GABBY *step up alongside* LUCKY.)

NATHANIEL. Oh, did we fail to mention we had a secret weapon?

GABBY. Hey there, baby. I missed you.

>   (GABBY *goes to kiss* LUCKY, *but he stops her.*)

JESS. No, he's under some kind of Skin Walker spell. Lucky, you can fight this! Lucky? Lucky, can you hear me?

LUCKY. (*Feigning confusion.*) J-J-Jess?

JESS. It's me, buddy. It's me.

LUCKY. I know. And this is me.

>   (LUCKY *reveals one of his hands that now has claws.*)

JESS. What?

>   (LUCKY *slashes* JESS *in the gut.*)

MALCOLM. NOOO!

LUCKY. I'm sorry. That has to hurt.

(JESS *is bleeding profusely.*)

MALCOLM. Come on, cuddles. I know you're inside there. Fight this off.

LUCKY. Hey, dummy.

Can I let you onto a little secret?

The guy you're trying to reach isn't here...cause the thing is, drum-roll...he never existed.

MALCOLM. What?

LUCKY. Thank you, ladies and gentlemen – boys and girls, the role of the powerless BFF has been played admirably by yours truly.

NATHANIEL. Isn't Chief Walker just awesome?

MALCOLM. What? You're Chief Walker?

LUCKY. I have to admit, Officer Malcolm, when you first joined us, I really was worried you'd recognize me.

(**LUCKY** *pulls out a bandana.*)

Who knew that a simple bandana could fool you so easily? You're like the Lois Lane of shitty cops. No wonder you couldn't make it in our merry band of superheroes. Luckily, your boyfriend here has made one badass lawman, don't you think?

NATHANIEL. I agree, I am pretty fucking awesome.

JESS. Lucky?

LUCKY. What's that, Jess?

JESS. We're going to kill you.

LUCKY. No offense, baby, but I don't believe you.

JESS. You said you loved me.

LUCKY. Who says I don't?

Everything that we experienced was real...barring a few white lies, my love for you is as real as raindrops.

JESS. You killed my sister.

LUCKY. Actually does your sister look dead?

GABBY. She does not.

LUCKY. Second, if I didn't care about you, you'd be a big ol' pile of yummy Jess-jerky right now for me and my crew here. But are you Jess-jerky?

GABBY. No, you are not.

LUCKY. The only thing that matters more to me than keeping Lost Vegas safe from Long Tooths is loving you, Jess December. You are my everything.

MALCOLM. I don't understand. If this is all you wanted, why hide who you were?

LUCKY. Isn't that answer obvious? I wanted to make sure the girl loved me for me.

JESS. Fuck you.

LUCKY. I understand you're angry, but let me ask you something simple. Do you miss seeing the stars at night?

Do you miss not being scared? Well, that's what I've done – that's the gift I gave your sister. The gift I'm gonna give you now.

JESS. This is a gift?

LUCKY. I created The Devils to save this town and though my methods may seem questionable, make no mistake, that's exactly what I've done. You are all safe because of me – because of what I've made.

MALCOLM. You actually think you're the good guys here.

LUCKY. Aren't we?

When's the last time either one of you seen a Long Tooth in these parts? That's right. You're welcome.

MALCOLM. Piss off!

LUCKY. Can you please shut him up now? I'm still talking to my girl here.

NATHANIEL. My pleasure.

Come here, cutie!

(*NATHANIEL kisses MALCOLM.*)

LUCKY. Not like that.

NATHANIEL. You never let me have any fun.

(**NATHANIEL** *pulls out a handkerchief and gags* **MALCOLM**.)

Just like old times, huh, love?

LUCKY. So I gotta ask, can you love me now that you really know me? Is that possible? Could we be together?

JESS. I'd die before I let that happen.

LUCKY. Are you sure?

(**JESS** *spits at* **LUCKY**.)

Fine. Be that way. You are right about one thing. You are gonna die.

(**LUCKY** *signals for* **GABBY** *to come over.*)

Gabby baby, why don't you show your sister how much you love her.

JESS. No. No, Gabs, don't.

GABBY. "Go to sleep, hon. I got this. No bad guys are gonna get you tonight. I promise."

(**GABBY** *chomps down on* **JESS**. *Bloods spews everywhere.*)

JESS. AAAAAGH!!

MALCOLM. Mmmph!

(*After* **JESS** *passes out from the pain,* **LUCKY** *stops* **GABBY**.)

LUCKY. That's good. She'll wake up a new person come morning.

(*After feeding on* **JESS**, **GABBY** *gets up a bit dazed.*)

Hey. You okay?

GABBY. What?

LUCKY. You with me?

GABBY. Huh?

LUCKY. HEY!

GABBY. Jason?

LUCKY. Stop acting retarded. Are you with me?

GABBY. Yeah. Yes. It's just – being near her...it's so weird.

LUCKY. Okay, maybe Skin Walker incest is a bad idea. Duly noted.

MALCOLM. Mmphf. Mmmmphf!

LUCKY. Officer Price! Looks like you haven't gotten any better at your job since you left it.

Jess is dead.

And it looks like she's gonna be hungry when she wakes up.

Hopefully she likes dark meat.

Come on, good guys, we've been way too nice in this town.

Time to remind everyone why we're called The Devils.

> (**LUCKY** *ties on his bandana and leads his people out to rampage.*)
>
> (*Cut to…*)
>
> (*Shadow sequence:*)
>
> (*In a shadow puppet sequence, we see* **LUCKY**, **GABBY**, *and* **NATHANIEL** *begin wreaking havoc in Lost Vegas. Buildings burn, citizens are beaten, havoc runs amok.*)

(*Voiceover.*) Alright, you assholes! It's been a minute since we Devils have rode through your town. Seems like you idiots need some reminding of the rules. No one goes outside at night. No one attempts to leave this town. And no one, under any circumstance, is allowed to kill any member of The Devils. Since two of my beloved Devils have died here on this evening, I must sadly punish all of you. Please do not make me do this again!

> (*The sequence crescendos as the town burns.*)

Interlude

(Projection: One year earlier...)

(Lights up on **DON DIEGO**. *He's packing his bags.)*

LUCKY. Hello. Are you Don Diego de la Vega?

DON DIEGO. I am. Have you heard of me?

LUCKY. I am a huge fan.

DON DIEGO. You must be Jessica's *amigo*, no?

LUCKY. That is correct. But you do know "Jess" isn't actually short for Jessica.

DON DIEGO. Is it not?

LUCKY. No, her parents were crazy religious. Her sis was named Gabriel and Jess was named, well, Jesus.

DON DIEGO. As in the Christ?

LUCKY. Yep, after Bleedy McHoly Hands himself.

DON DIEGO. Then like the great Jesus, let us hope she can be the savior this town needs.

LUCKY. Yeah, that's actually what I going to talk to you about. It's really not good that you filled her head with all this "fighting *Los Diablos*" nonsense.

DON DIEGO. *Los Diablos* killed her sister. She deserves her vengeance.

LUCKY. *Los Diablos* saved this town, Mister. Her sister's fine. But now you just made it super awkward for everybody involved.

DON DIEGO. I see. This is jealousy you speak of. I assure you that you have nothing to fear from me. Though I am exceptionally handsome, I have no interest in your *señorita*. I love another. Though she is gone from this Earth, she remains...in my heart.

LUCKY. Oh right. Cathcrine. She was quite...what's the word?

DON DIEGO. How do you know about my Catherine? I did not say anything about her.

LUCKY. Delicious. That's the word.

DON DIEGO. *Diablo!*

> (**DON DIEGO** *raises his cane like a weapon.*)

My name is Don Diego De La Vega. You killed my lover. Prepare to die!

> (**DON DIEGO** *attacks* **LUCKY** *with his cane.*)
>
> (*It smashes against his body, but doesn't budge him.*)

Well, that didn't seem to be very effective, did it?

LUCKY. Let me try.

> (**LUCKY** *pulls out a knife and stabs* **DON DIEGO** *in the gut.*)
>
> (**DON DIEGO** *falls to the grounds, writhes in pain, and then abruptly "dies."*)
>
> (*As* **LUCKY** *begins to leave…*)

DON DIEGO. *El Diablo!*

Wait.

> (*The wounded* **DON DIEGO** *peels himself off the ground and faces* **LUCKY** *again.*)
>
> (**DON DIEGO** *attacks.* **LUCKY** *dodges and stabs* **DON DIEGO** *again in the chest.*)
>
> (**DON DIEGO** *collapses again "dead."*)
>
> (*As* **LUCKY** *leaves.*)

Wait.

> (**LUCKY** *walks back and before* **DON DIEGO** *can even get off the ground,* **LUCKY** *stabs him three times in the gut as* **DON DIEGO** *screams in pain.*)
>
> (**DON DIEGO** *collapses again.* **LUCKY** *kicks at his body to see if he's actually dead.* **DON DIEGO** *doesn't move.*)
>
> (*Satisfied,* **LUCKY** *begins to leave again.*)

Wait.

LUCKY. No more waiting.

> (**LUCKY** *tosses his knife across the stage and it impales* **DON DIEGO***'s head.*)
>
> (**DON DIEGO** *dies for real.*)

Five

(Projection: Chapter Five: Dead girl talking.)

(Projection: Present.)

(Lights up on **MALCOLM** *waking up and finding a feral* **JESS** *chewing on something dead. Her hair is wild and she's all crouched over like an animal.)*

MALCOLM. *(Muffled.)* Oh fuck. Oh fuck oh fuck fuck fuck fuck.

> *(She violently turns to* **MALCOLM** *and rushes at him.)*

(Muffled.) Oh God!

> *(But she stops herself and just stares at him.)*

JESS. Mal…colm?

MALCOLM. *(Muffled.)* Jess?

JESS. What. The. FUCK?! Am I dead? This is so weird.

MALCOLM. *(Muffled.)* Uh-huh, but, um, how come you're not killing me?

JESS. I don't know. Why aren't I killing you?

MALCOLM. *(Muffled.)* You're still you?

JESS. Yes. I'm still me. Mentally speaking. But…

MALCOLM. *(Muffled.)* You're dead.

JESS. I'm dead. Yeah. That's not good.

MALCOLM. *(Muffled.)* Yo, how's that possible?

JESS. How should I know?

MALCOLM. *(Muffled.)* Well, you are all demonically magical now, maybe you can summon some of that demon magic to figure some shit out.

JESS. I am connected to something bigger – larger than myself – and it's telling me that I should probably eat you right now. But I won't. But you do smell yummy. (Don't eat him, Jess. Don't eat him.) Ah, one little bite can't hurt.

> *(***JESS*** *goes to bite* **MALCOLM** *in the face, but stops.)*

Just kidding.

(She ungags and unties him.)

MALCOLM. Yo, that's messed up.

JESS. Maybe it's a slow process. Maybe I'll want to kill you later. But don't worry – I'm vegan. If I have the willpower to deny the delicious aroma of bacon, then I have the willpower to deny pretty much anything.

MALCOLM. Whatever it is, I'm just glad you're not killing me right now.

JESS. Or maybe…

*(**JESS** opens up her shirt to show her tooth necklace.)*

It wouldn't have anything to do with this, would it?

MALCOLM. Where'd you get that?

JESS. Don Diego de la Vega.

MALCOLM. The Fox?

JESS. You know him?

*(**MALCOLM** open his own shirt to reveal the same necklace.)*

So this IS magical?

MALCOLM. What? No. Why would it be magical? Just cause I'm black, it's got to be magical?

JESS. Sorry.

MALCOLM. I'm just joshing ya, it's totally magical.

JESS. Really?

MALCOLM. No.

JESS. What?

MALCOLM. Yes.

JESS. You clearly know Don Diego.

MALCOLM. Well, that explains why you're not completely nutters right now.

JESS. No, it doesn't.

How the hell is this necklace keeping me sane?

MALCOLM. You do know what kind of teeth those are, right?

Those are Long Tooth's...teeth.

(From the distance, there's screams and the sounds of panic and disorder.)

JESS. The city's burning.

MALCOLM. It's time to end this.

JESS. Are you ready?

MALCOLM. Go look for your sister, I'm going to go make nice with my ex.

JESS. Good luck.

MALCOLM. You too.

(Smash cut to...)

MALCOLM. Nathaniel!

NATHANIEL. Why hello there, love. If you're still here amongst the walking, it must mean our great master plan has went to shit. No big surprise. Our good boy Chief Walker is definitely not thinking with his right head these days.

MALCOLM. What's happened to you?

NATHANIEL. What's happened to me? What's happened to you?

You used to be all sorts of fun, but now look at you – you look like a malnourished Aaron Neville after a weekend in a leather club.

MALCOLM. What?

NATHANIEL. Right. You never get any of my references. I used to really feel self-conscious about that, but now – not so much.

MALCOLM. Can you not joke right now?

NATHANIEL. I'm just trying to lighten the mood, love.

You know, for being a top, you are exceptionally anal.

MALCOLM. Stop.

NATHANIEL. I've missed you, Malcolm.

MALCOLM. Don't say that.

NATHANIEL. Say what? The truth?

MALCOLM. If you really meant it, you would let me save you.

NATHANIEL. Save me? How could you possibly save me? I saved this town. All of it.

MALCOLM. I can save your soul.

NATHANIEL. My soul? Right. That again. You still haven't accepted the fact I'm a Skin Walker.

There's no bringing me back. This is who I am. This is who I've always wanted to be.

MALCOLM. No. I can. I've found a way –

NATHANIEL. What? With that magic necklace you have there?

Oh, you didn't think I knew about it, did you?

It's okay, love. Come on. Let's try it on.

> (MALCOLM *cautiously approaches* NATHANIEL *and places the necklace on him.*)
>
> (*Something magical happens.* NATHANIEL *opens his eyes.*)

Oh God. My word. I feel... Walker's control is gone. I'm fixed! I'm cured! I haven't felt this good in years. Let's...go...kill...everyone.

MALCOLM. What?

NATHANIEL. Oh. Not everybody. Just the bad people. But, honestly, isn't everybody just a little bad inside. Thusly why we should kill them all.

MALCOLM. It's not working.

NATHANIEL. Actually, it's working just fine, luv. It gives a Skin Walker back the control of their mind. And so it has... Walker has no control of me now. However, the rest of all this IS me.

MALCOLM. You've gone completely mad.

NATHANIEL. Perhaps I have. There's just so much death one can inflict until their heart completely dies.

MALCOLM. Nathan.

NATHANIEL. But worry not, luv, there is still one itty bitty sane thought still intact inside my soul. The one thing that tortures me so. Do you know what that is?

MALCOLM. I don't know if I want to.

NATHANIEL. That thing is…you. Even with this blood thirst inside me, I still love you.

MALCOLM. Don't.

NATHANIEL. I do, Malcolm. As mad as my madness can be, those feelings have never left. If anything, they've only grown. Be with me. Screw these breeders. Let them have this fight – let them kill each other for all I care. Because if they did, this would be all ours. For the rest of our days, you and I could be kings…and at night, I would be your queen.

MALCOLM. Don't look at me like that.

NATHANIEL. Like what?

MALCOLM. Like that. Like you still care. Don't make that face.

NATHANIEL. You used to like this face.

MALCOLM. Yeah, and you used to be vegan.

NATHANIEL. Malcolm. I do care. Very much.

MALCOLM. Nathaniel.

NATHANIEL. Shhhh.

> (**NATHANIEL** *grabs* **MALCOLM** *and kisses him hard.*)

MALCOLM. I'm sorry.

NATHANIEL. Why?

> (**MALCOLM** *stabs* **NATHANIEL.**)

REALLY?! Are you kidding me?

After I just spilled out my heart, you went off and stabbed me? What kind of unromantic asshole are you?

MALCOLM. You aren't him. The Nathaniel I fell in love with is not a murdering psychopath.

NATHANIEL. Well, we can't all be perfect.

  (MALCOLM pulls out his sword.)

MALCOLM. We both chose our paths. You knew that at some point they'd cross again.

NATHANIEL. You promised me that you'd love me forever.

MALCOLM. And I do, man. But this isn't about love. This is about doing what's right.

  (NATHANIEL pulls out his own blade as well.)

NATHANIEL. Are we really going to do this?

MALCOLM. Yes.

NATHANIEL. Then how do I look?

MALCOLM. You look good.

NATHANIEL. Good luck.

MALCOLM. Same to you.

  (An elaborate fight ensues. Blades clash, wounds happen, both men are hurt.)

  (In the end, NATHANIEL is over MALCOLM with his sword.)

NATHANIEL. I can't.
I'm sorry I failed you.

  (NATHANIEL slowly raises his blade, which allows MALCOLM the opportunity to stab NATHANIEL in the heart.)

  (NATHANIEL grabs onto MALCOLM.)

Do it.

MALCOLM. What?

NATHANIEL. DO IT!

  (NATHANIEL goes to bite MALCOLM, which forces MALCOLM to slice NATHANIEL's throat.)

  (NATHANIEL grabs his wound and backs away.)

  (He manages a bloody smile.)

I'm glad you won, love.

(**NATHANIEL** *falls.*)

(*A burst of light and sound as* **NATHANIEL** *dies.*)

(*His body falls limp and lifeless.*)

(**MALCOLM**, *realizing what he's just done, grabs onto his fallen lover…*)

MALCOLM. No. NO no no no no! I take it back. I TAKE IT BACK! Please get up. Please. I'm sorry. I'm so sorry.

(*Cut to…*)

(*On either side of the stage,* **LUCKY** *along with* **GABBY** *meets a bloodied* **JESS**.)

LUCKY. Hey there, Jess. I see you're all awake now. How does it feel to finally be one of us? You must be hungry.

JESS. Yep.

(**JESS** *pulls out a gun and unloads three shots into* **LUCKY**'s *body.*)

LUCKY. Dumb bitch. Guns…can't…

(*He collapses off stage and falls with a thud.*)

GABBY. Jason!

JESS. Gabby. Hon. Listen to me –

GABBY. You shot Jason!

JESS. I did. But he's not –

GABBY. He gave us a gift and this is how you repay him?

JESS. You aren't thinking right.

GABBY. See! That's your problem, Jess. You always think you're smarter than me.

JESS. Because I AM smarter than you.

GABBY. Book smarts.

JESS. EVERYTHING smarts.

Am I the one who ran away, got caught by an evil demonic police force, and then got turned into a fucking werewolf? Ugh, dammit, I guess that's me too.

GABBY. I'm not a werewolf. I'm a Skin Walker. I can turn into all sorts of things.

Like a cat. Or a bunny. Or a really hungry gerbil.

JESS. What?

GABBY. What? That doesn't scare you? Well, I'm not really good at the magic transform-y part just yet, but I'm crazy good at the killing bitches part.

JESS. Come with me, Gabs. I can fix you.

GABBY. WHO SAID I WANT FIXING?!

(GABBY steps to JESS, JESS reflexively points her gun at her sister.)

Oh, okay. Whoa. Are you really gonna shoot me? Me? Your sissy? I really –

(GABBY suddenly kicks JESS in the gut and disarms her.)

– can't believe how stupid you are!

(GABBY goes to strike her again, but JESS avoids her.)

JESS. Don't make me fight you.

GABBY. You don't have to fight me. If you want, you can just stand there and let me beat the shit out of you. I'd actually prefer it. You're freakishly tall for someone sharing the same genetic makeup as myself.

(GABBY pulls out two long knives.)

Let's cut you down to size.

(Music like Marilyn Manson's cover of "SWEET DREAMS" fills the stage.)

(The two girls fight. It's an elaborate and badass battle, but one primarily consisting of GABBY attacking as JESS defends herself.)

(Eventually JESS is able to disarm GABBY. JESS puts down her own weapons which allow the two girls to get into an elaborate, no-holds barred capoeira fight.)

(Without the fear of killing GABBY, JESS unleashes hits and kicks on her sister.)

(The unrelenting barrage of hits finally knocks **GABBY** *on her ass.)*

(It looks like **JESS** *wins, until abruptly* **GABBY** *gets back up to her feet and smiles.)*

*(***MALCOLM*** *suddenly appears.)*

MALCOLM. Yeah, I keep on trying, but all this girl-on-girl action really just doesn't do it for me.

*(***MALCOLM*** *tosses the tooth necklace on* **GABBY** *which magically knocks her out.)*

JESS. Gabby!

MALCOLM. She'll be fine once she wakes up.

(Suddenly, the sounds of footsteps. Giant footsteps.)

JESS. What the hell is that?

MALCOLM. Wendigo.

(Badass thumping hip-hop infused Ennio Morricone-like music fills the space as a giant stage-sized monstrous **LUCKY** *(puppet) enters the stage and attacks.)*

(And in the greatest theatrical fight to ever be seen on any stage anywhere in the whole fucking universe, **MALCOLM** *and* **JESS** *fight the monstrous* **LUCKY**.*)*

(Theatrical tricks and stage magic abound, but in the end, both **JESS** *and* **MALCOLM** *are able to defeat the monster by simultaneously slicing its throat open.)*

(A huge light, sound, and multimedia explosion occurs as **LUCKY** *the Wendigo dies.)*

(The world returns to normal.)

*(***GABBY*** *wakes up.)*

GABBY. Jess?

JESS. Gabby!

*(***JESS*** *runs to her sister's side.)*

GABBY. Where am I? What happened?

JESS. It doesn't matter. All that matters is you're here now. I love you.

> *(The two girls hug.)*
>
> *(MALCOLM looks at the fallen LUCKY and tries to quietly exit.)*

Hey! Where are you going?

MALCOLM. My business here is finished.

JESS. So you're just going to go?

MALCOLM. There's nothing left for me. Nothing at all.

JESS. Well then do you mind if we join you?

MALCOLM. …

JESS. …

MALCOLM. Yeah. I could use the company.

> *(JESS walks up to hug MALCOLM, it looks like she's going to kiss him though.)*

Hey! What are you doing? I told you I'm gay.

JESS. I'm hugging you, dummy. Gay people do hug.

> *(MALCOLM and JESS hug.)*
>
> *(Suddenly…)*

DINGO. *(Offstage.)* JESS DECEMBER! I'M CALLING YOU OUT!

> *(DINGO enters the stage.)*

You killed my brothers. Now prepare to –

> *(She quickly draws her sidearm and shoots him. He falls dead.)*

MALCOLM. You do know that doesn't actually kill them, right?

JESS. Yeah.

Whatever.

I'll finish him later.

Guess that's that.

(**JESS** *looks at her empty gun and drops it.*)
(*The three heroes leave the stage as lights fade.*)

End of Play